REVIEW

The future holds secrets unknown to us. It is best we live our lives treating others with respect. This is the essence of the message in Mafemba's All Bets are Off.

Chipo Musikavanhu – Author, Dews from the East

ABOUT THE AUTHOR

Talent Chipiwa Mafemba is a young lady who is goal driven and aspires to let known unto the world her thoughts through her writing. Born in the country of Zimbabwe, I grew up in the city of Harare, attended my primary school at Louis Mountbatten Primary School, did my 'O' Level at Lydia Chimonyo Girls High School and did my 'A' Level at Kwekwe High School. I hold a Bachelor of Nursing degree from University of Witwatersrand and I'm currently a fulltime Midwife. Writing as is reading is my escape hobby. It helps me as I take a break from the busy life of being a nurse and it is an opportunity for me to get in touch with who I am. Through my writing it is my desire to give my readers entertainment, inspiration, motivation and wise words that are informative.

All bets are off

A novella

Chipiwa Talent Mafemba

Cover Design, Copyright © 2019, by Farai Macheka.

First Edition.

This novel is a work of fiction. Names, characters, places, and incidents either are the product of the author's imagination or are used fictitiously. Any resemblance to actual events, locales, organizations, or persons living or dead is entirely coincidental and beyond the intent of either the author or the publisher.

No parts of this publication may be reproduced, stored in a retrieval system or transmitted in any form by any means, electronic, mechanical, photocopying, recording, or otherwise without prior permission from the author. The only exception is brief quotations in printed reviews.

Independently published, U.S.A.

Copyright © 2019 Chipiwa Mafemba
All rights reserved.
ISBN: 978-1-69293-132-2

DEDICATION

To all the young people who are yet to be capable subjects of the highs and lows of love. <3

CONTENTS

	Preface	xi
	Acknowledgments	xiii
1	Loss of both, rejuvenation of self	15
2	Tears on the bus	24
3	Who is he?	32
4	The art of letting go	38
5	The Rev's call	45
6	To save the marriage or not?	53
7	Happy Anniversary!!	61
8	What is going on with Sheila?	68
9	The warmth of a mother's love	74
10	A bolt from the blue	83

PREFACE

Falling in love is daring as the outcome is often unpredictable. What is more, even better is falling for the right person as it is fulfilling and rewarding. The challenge comes with the predicament of realising that the fairy-tale could have possibly be an illusion. It is in addressing this challenge that many end up with a misinterpretation of falling in love. For some the disheartening experience draws them to avoidance of falling in love and in extreme cases, some people will prefer to disengage in any form of relationship.

Nonetheless, it is important to remember that falling wrong happens but it can also pass. Healing is a process that is worth admitting to as it detoxifies the soul and the spirit from any negativity engrained by the hurt. It relieves off the baggage acquired from the affliction. To appreciate love, healing from being hurt is of great essence. I wrote this with the young people in mind, intending to encourage them that the course of falling in love is amazing as much as it is unpredictable. In the event of the relationship being on the fritz it is not the close of age so do not be disheartened. That which is not for you let it pass, such that when you are free from the gaffe you have the chance to fall in love with the right person.

To the reader, this book will present a storyline which is relatable. As you visualize it, you are likely going to try and put the puzzle pieces into place that will lead you into drawing a conclusion. To have the correct and complete piece of the story, reading this book will be of essence as the storyline contains interesting enclosed content.

ACKNOWLEDGMENTS

I would like to extend my appreciation and love to my parents Beatrice and Alban together with my siblings Avril, Simbarashe and my brother in-law Langton for the unending support and encouragement.

1 LOSS OF BOTH, REJUVENATION OF SELF

"I've been struggling to come up with a name for our unborn baby," Stacy said, as she attempted to sit on the green grass of the park.

Timmy stretched out his hand upward. In a gentleman gesture, he supported his heavily gravidarum paramour. "There we go—see I got you my love," he said, glaring at her with a flicker in his eyes accompanied by a smile.

Unaware of how to hide from his piercing stare, she let down her face and fixed her gaze on her belly. When she was bronzed and roasting hot from blushing, she broke the silence with a question. "Wow, oh really? So are you going to sit and look at me like that all day, I mean, I know you admire all this that I am….," she said with a simper and sarcastically rolling her eyes. "...but let's save it for another day, today we need to focus on finding a name for our precious gift," she continued, looking at her hand as she rubbed her belly effortlessly. On remembering that she had brought him packed lunch, at once she dug into her bag with the other hand and handed it out to him.

Timmy enjoyed her sandwiches so she had made it a tradition to always pack them in a lunch tin so he could delightedly help himself whenever they met. Upon having the first bite, Timmy closed his eyes, smiled and nodded. In the two years of their courtship he had shown appreciation for her cooking by showering her with newfangled compliments at every presenting opportunity. "Clearly, with no doubt you prepare savoury food."

As usual she was ready to hear what new flattering comment he had for her. She could not hide her smile.

"You know my love, I think I've an idea," Timmy said, with veritable gladness and excitement on his face. "What about Cadeau, I suggest we could name our baby Cadeau! Yes."

Dazed, she glared at him and with a grin she tried suppressing her laughter but it got the better out of her and she spurt a loud laugh.

All this kept on replaying in her mind, the picture so raw as if it were only yesterday when Timmy and she had all the love that the universe could ever offer two people in a commitment. It had been three years since Stacy lost her first love to an arranged marriage by his parents. They had both tried to contend it in the name of their unborn baby but unfortunately Stacy miscarried. On the third night of her third trimester, she had woken up in the middle of the night feeling cramps in her lower abdomen and her linen soaked with blood. She had wasted no time and informed her roommate. Her roommate overwhelmed at what she had seen ran to seek help to take Stacy to the hospital. It was at the hospital where she ascertained that she had encountered cervical insufficiency which compromised accommodation of the foetus in her womb.

Stacy was directed into the office; she sat in there waiting for the church head warden who was going to see her regarding the post she had applied for. As she waited, she could feel her heart racing fast. The silence of the unfamiliar surroundings added to her state of unease. She remembered how at one instance she had encountered a similar discomfort; it was in the hospital.

Aunty Martha, the St Johns Anglican Church administrator for at least three decades had taken the decision to retire due to the challenges she began facing with her geriatric comorbidities. The advertising of the vacancy on the chapel's notice board was as a result of her stepping down. Stacy's mother and Aunty Martha were long-term friends and she was aware of Stacy's challenge with getting a job. Stacy had been submitting her Curriculum Vitae to different companies in search of a job to no avail for the past three years. Aunty Martha had advised Stacy to apply for the post.

Even though she was overeducated for it, the job

would be a good start for her in place of being idle. Idleness had done nothing short of belittling her. She had failed to achieve anything tangible after the loss of her baby and her first love, Timmy. This experience had scarred her, causing her to make the decision of detaching herself from being involved in any form of companionship. She was scared of being let down again. It would strip her off the residual sentiments left of her sense of self. Her priority was to focus on improving her sense of self-worth in substitute for seeking companionship. Finding a job would keep her occupied and destruct her from wondering.

After losing Cadeau, Stacy and Timmy had met and had an obdurate conversation.

"You need to understand that Cadeau was the only hope that we had to evidently challenge my parents. Not that I blame you my love but we have lost our precious gift and there's nothing else that I can possibly say or do that will be able to convince my parents." He had held her shoulder trying to console her as she sobbed extensively and he continued, "Stacy there isn't anything we can do at this point."

"Tell your parents Timmy that you love me. If it's a marriage how can one be in a union with someone they don't know? You don't even know her Timmy, how will you be able to love her? A union is to be built on and supported by a firm foundation of authentic love and that's what we have."

"You don't understand Stacy, it's more complicated than it seems and an excuse based on our love only won't suffice. Love with no evidence of a fixed entity has no voice," heartbrokenly responded Timmy in a strident deep voice. He had also been hurt that his parents had objected his decision to marry Stacy. However, it had been important for him to be in a marriage blessed by his parents. He loved Stacy but because of the situation he had decided to not go ahead with his will to marry her for any resulting estranged relationship between him and his parents would have haunted her. He had to be strong and void their relationship; they had run out of solutions to save it. Unbearable as it was his conscience registered a feeling of guilt, it had not been easy for him especially upon watching how Stacy had broken down. He would never forgive himself for putting her through so much pain. In spite of this, he had to repress his feelings and deal with the dilemma at once.

"I can't believe this, so you are telling me you have given up and you'll no longer hold on to what we have built in these past years?"

Someone's entry into the office awakened her from her horrendous flashback to facing reality.

"Good morning ma'am," said a middle aged gentleman who had entered into the office.

At once reality struck; it was now her chance to make her tomorrow better. Messing up this opportunity would mean more years of idleness and aimless job hunting. I am going to make the most of this opportunity, she said to herself as she stood up, extending her hand to greet back the gentleman. "Good morning to you too sir, my name is …"

"Stacy, right and you're here regarding the

interview for the chapel administration position," he said walking around the office desk to take his seat.

He knew her already, if anything, that was overwhelming because if he already knew her then he would have expectations of her in the interview. If she failed to sell herself to meet his expectations it could be the end of her, she would be doomed. "Yes, that's right. I'm Stacy. I saw an advertisement for the vacancy on the chapel's notice board and I was interested so I immediately applied for it".

She was saying more than she was supposed to. He did not need her to give all that information and her knees where knocking each other. Upon noticing this Reverend Paine raised his left hand in a gesture directing her to let herself sit. "Please help yourself."

Stacy thanked him and took a seat; suddenly her nerves withered instantly and she resumed to a calmer state. She briefly closed her eyes, prayed a short prayer thanking God for the regained calmness. If her nervousness had continued it would have drained her focus. She took a deep breath then opened her eyes. She looked up and saw that he had his head hunched down into the drawers focusing on the papers he was assembling. Luckily, he had not been watching her do all her mindfulness exercises. Then again the papers, they definitely would have the list of questions he ought to ask her. Why was it taking him so long? It could only mean there was so much he wanted to ask her. Before she knew it, she was in deep anxiety going through fear of the unknown. Was he going to ask her for years of experience? If he was, she was going to be embarrassed. How was she going to explain to him three plain years of unemployment? Would this render her inexperienced and incompatible for the job? On and on she wondered, her imagination projecting her towards the negative.

Finally, Reverend Paine found all he was looking for; he placed a mass of the papers on his desk and looked at Stacy with an assuring and friendly look. "Pardon my manners I didn't introduce myself. I'm Reverend Paine the St Johns Anglican Cathedral head of the clergy. Please allow yourself to relax we won't have anything intense. May you please present to me the required documents mentioned on the job advertisement."

From her plastic portfolio she withdrew her identity document, high school examination certificate, Human Resources Management degree transcript plus certificate, C.I.S professional qualification certificate, curriculum vitae, police clearance and medical report. A formal referral letter had been listed as a requirement but she didn't have one, neither did she mention it to him as she handed to him the papers. She had no idea how to say it as it would be embarrassing. So she thought it would be rather better if he would figure it out himself.

"I see that it's been three years since you left school. Have you been employed anywhere in these three years?"

"No sir," Stacy responded sensing a feeling of disappointment. But it had not been her fault, she had tried her very best to hunt for a job. Perhaps she ought to justify herself so she continued, "But I did try to look for a job only to no avail. I'm hoping that I'd be able to get an opportunity to have my first job here and with determination I promise I'll put my skills to practice".

She did it again, she was saying more than she was supposed to; his question did not need her to give all that information. Amused by her response he nodded in agreement with a smile on his face. "Impressive. You mention that you're hoping. That's good to have hope, it keeps us all going. However, I've taken a good look at your documents and your filled in application form following being strongly advised by Ms. Martha that you were most suitable for this post. She mentioned to me more regarding your character and she tried to convince me to give you a chance at this."

He was taking too long to tell her the outcome. With her heart racing fast she became restless and struggled to sit still as she was constantly fidgeting. Impatience gave her the courage to look straight at him.

With a smile of reassurance, he continued, "On behalf of the clergy and administration team I would like to congratulate you on being our new administrator. With me on this desk are the forms that you need to sign in when we have completed discussing your contract terms and conditions."

Excited she stood up to thank the gentleman. At last, dawn to her dusk, she finally had a job. A relief from her idle life, the intensity of her excitement was untold, it even exhausted all the energy she had. Immediately she reverted to her seat, it all seemed like a dream. At long last she was making progress. The past three years her life had seemed to be on a standstill only waiting for this breakthrough. This thought hit her hard and her eyes could not contain her tears.

Just then Aunty Martha knocked and entered the office. She knew that Stacy would get the job but knew not that this offer would overwhelm her to such an extent.

"Good morning my dear, Stacy here is going through an emotional phase of excitement, would you mind attending to her?"

"Good morning Father, that's all right," she said as she walked towards poor Stacy. "Oh my dear Stacy, come on don't you cry now," she said embracing Stacy.

"Okay then, I'll leave you two at it. Congratulations to you my dear; will see you soon and thank you for coming through for us Ma Martha. May the peace of the Lord continue to be with you. Have a blessed day."

"Thank you!" chorused Aunty Martha and Stacy at their exit.

2 TEARS ON THE BUS

Aunty Martha took a few days to orient Stacy on the working dynamics in reference to her scope of duties around the cathedral before she left.

Stacy learnt well and quickly that she managed to promptly get the hang of things around. It had been a while since she had felt that she was leading a purposeful life. Her contribution to her family was beyond financial aid, she now also gave informative advice which she had absorbed from watching the Reverend counselling. Congregation members would come seeking his knowledgeable advice and counselling on their diverse life confrontations. The environment contributed to her spiritual and mental growth as she was getting exposed to different situations and life challenges that people encountered.

She became aware of so many innovative facts of life. One of them being 'life has as many ups as it has downs for everyone'. She also realized that focusing on the challenges only allowed for time to be wasted.

Whereas choosing to focus on identifying the positive aspects present in any misfortune could help realise the positive outcome that could arise from it. It was only then when she was able to peacefully recall the sequence of events on the loss of her unborn baby and Timmy. No longer would the memories put her in grief or aggression, her healing was finally definite.

She was assigned a new task; facilitation of charity projects. These projects were a norm especially during the festive season where charity is a culture in Christianity. Unfamiliarity with some of the duties that would be required of her hardly frightened her as she was reassured that the whole clergy and administration team would be actively involved to ensure a good outcome of the projects. Stacy had to accompany various groups of company representatives who were donating to the Anglican ministry homes. Therefore, she, the delegated reverend, the project planner and a group of company representatives would have to mobilize and go to each and every Anglican home within the city.

In a fortnight they had successfully attended to most of the homes including old people's care facilities, children's homes and the disabled people's facility.

It was the disabled people's home that stood out the most for her. It was a terrifying and traumatic encounter. Devastating thoughts clouded her as she wondered how one was possibly able to survive with the impairments she saw. Out of all the impairments, being quadriplegic stood out the most. The majority had been diagnosed with cerebral palsy from birth and others had motor vehicle accidents post effects. At the sight of them, in different ages, the elderly, adults and infants, she was filled with sadness, agony, pity, hurt and helplessness. To avoid causing a scene, she excused herself and left for the tour bus. Unable to contain the devastating thoughts, she gushed into a fount of tears once she sat on one of the bus seats. *Unable to feed themselves they rely on the caregiver's assistance. The same applies to them needing to use the toilet and to each and every one of their activities of daily living. They live dependent lives, relying on someone's assistance. It is unthinkable how it feels for them, to live relying on assistance. It is possible that they feel helpless and trapped in their own bodies. What of the caregivers? How have they managed to cope with the load of attending to each of their needs?*

"Are you all right," asked a male voice.

She was startled as she was unaware of anyone's presence in the bus. This made her feel embarrassed, but then responded, "Oh, I'm sorry," she said, wiping off tears from her cheeks. "I didn't mean to alarm you. I had no idea someone had been left behind in the bus. Don't mind me at all. I'll be okay."

"It's all right, you don't have to apologise. I'd just come to collect this box; we figured we were one box short."

With a phony smile she looked at him, "Sure, you may go ahead don't let me be in your way." *Tears are believed to be a sign of weakness, not only is it embarrassing for some men to be seen crying but same also applies to some women too. It's been long since I last cried like this. I used to despise my tears; they used to make me feel vulnerable. Astoundingly this time around I don't feel vulnerable. Rather I feel my tears are in sort of communication to how I feel internally. They are an outward expression of my present inward emotions. In addition, they also vent a message to me of gratefulness. I had so much that I had not paid attention to and had disregarded things which another person would have appreciated such as my ability to walk around and sit independently.*

After the bus incident, she encouraged herself to be more mindful, to pay attention in detail to all that she had and also appreciate it. With every task, came a new lesson. Growth came from learning; Stacy learnt more than she had expected.

A few weeks into the new year, Reverend Paine passed through her office as he was heading for a parish meeting. "Good morning Stacy, this afternoon there's going to be a person from Qadar Company who will pass by to collect the recorded minutes of our visits to the Anglican Homes last season. I pray you've them compiled and ready."

"Good morning; yes all the data is compiled and ready Father."

"Good job, so please do assist for I unfortunately will not be around. The men's forum meeting for the parish begins in the next hour and it can't be predicted how long it may take."

"You need not worry yourself Sir as I'll do what you've asked and won't let you down."

She had impressed the Reverend with her excellent work ethic; he was reassured of the decision he had made to recruit her following Martha's recommendation and advice.

Drained and exhausted from her dreadful hectic day, she patiently waited for the day to end. All the day's work was done except that the person whom

Reverend had mentioned had not come yet. There was a knock on the door.

'Finally!' She sighed. "Please enter," she said collecting the files with the minutes, budget and statistics records, ready to hand them over.

A commendable handsome gentleman with a well figured masculine frame walked in. He wore a grey cotton squared-off collar classic shirt, which fit him so well it gave an instant appeal. The sleeves of his shirt were neatly rolled up three quarters of his arm. The rest of his lower physique was covered in complementary flat-front pants. Age assumption, early thirties, fairly attractive and seemed familiar too.

A while ago she had been keenly looking forward to going home ready to immediately dump the files into the hands of the collector and leave but it was only because she was not expecting the collector to be looking as attractive. It had been a while since she had felt this enticed, making it seem awkward for her. Tongue tied, she thought to herself she would not have minded waiting for longer if she had known to be expecting him.

Upon entering the room, he hastily strode towards her. For a minute he stood waiting for her to initiate the conversation with a greeting, but she kept staring at him. Perhaps she was cross with him.

"Good afternoon," he said with a charming grin. "Please accept my apologies for being late. I got caught up on my way. I'm really sorry for causing you any inconveniences."

"Don't you worry. I totally understand and it's okay, I appreciate your apology, please help yourself," she responded, startled from her admiration of him and gestured him to the chair. Aware of the reason he had come, out of courtesy she asked, "How may I be of assistance to you Mr...?"

"Firstly may I be honest with you, I'm really glad to see you glowing, nothing would please me more than to get to know you ma'am."

Immediately Stacy began developing a dislike for the poor fellow; she was blustered by his over familiarity.

"With all due respect Sir, my job and the reason why you found me still here, I assist people who walk in with what they need or instruct them to where they can get further help. So please, kindly allow me firstly to do my delegated task," she said in a frank and gentle voice. Smiling, she continued, "And my name is Stacy, thank you".

Not taking into account her precision he replied, "Oh nice to meet you Stacy, I'm Robin but you can just call me Rob like most people do."

"Likewise, Rob," she said getting a bit impatient and eager to have their meeting over.

Noticing how she was growing edgy, "I'm sorry," he said, "...for anything I said that came across as offensive to you or that made you angry. It's just that I remember you from the last time we met, if by any chance you recall. It was in the tour bus and you were in sort of a state, not well at all."

They had met before! In the tour bus, he mentioned; she definitely did not recall seeing him. There were a number of young men with whom she had shared trips during the period of facilitating the charity projects. He might have known her prior but still that was no justification for how over familiar he had begun. He clearly enjoyed charming his way through women. Unfortunately, no luck for him with Stacy. "Rob you say? I really would like to remember but unfortunately I don't. Once again how may I possibly be of help to you?"

"Very well, I'm here on behalf of the Qadar Company; assigned to collect the compiled data on the home visits we participated in during the festive season. We need it for…"

Before he could complete explaining Stacy slid a small file across the table to him. "There you are. It's all here. I'm sure you certainly will put these to good use." Stacy started packing up and tidying up the office ready to leave hoping he would see that as his cue to leave. To her surprise, unbothered, still seating he kept starring at her. After a while, she began to feel uncomfortable and could not stand his starring any longer. Politely she said, "Is there anything else, you'd like Mr. Robin?"

Robin continuously looking at her smiled simultaneously and then said, "Well yes, I'd like to ask, why you have such a feisty character?"

She was annoyed by his question; he certainly knew how to step on Stacy's toes. At this point he had gone way over bounds. She had not expected her day to end like this; so much drama. Although he had asked such a truthful question which, she was aware of but had worked on perfectly concealing. She just looked at him unaware of how to possibly answer him.

Conscious of her being speechless, he continued, "I see it seems to be a long story and I understand. You don't have to explain if you don't wish to. Each of us has fought or is fighting a battle through life. You seem to be an amazing person, Stacy, although I can't help but wonder how much battle you've fought to impact you so; is that what made you cry at the home of the disabled people?"

It was then when she suddenly remembered, he was the man that saw her crying in the tour bus; how could she have forgotten him! "Oh the bus, that's where we met before. I don't know how I possibly missed that indeed, we've met before."

"At least you recall. If I may confess, throughout that week as I was observing you, I was amazed by your work ethic. However, with you being overly drowned in work I never got the chance to have a chat with you. When an opportunity presented itself, you seemed to be in a state of despair."

"Despair you say, I'm really amazed because I had no idea that I've a predictable character. It sounds as if you've studied me way too much."

"I hope that impresses you."

"No. Not at all. Rather scary. Actually, it's so weird. So were you really getting the box or you saw me heading for the bus?"

"Ask no questions hear no lies", Rob responded and they both laughed.

3 WHO IS HE?

When Timmy had held her in his arms that was the only moment at which she had felt butterflies in her stomach. On every instance that she had met up with Robin, the sight of him had rejuvenated that feeling. Gradually she let down her guard; there had to be something peculiar about Robin which made her feel this way as no other except Timmy had made her feel like that.

Indisputably a part of her got worn out when Timmy left; time heals and meeting Robin too had enabled her restoration of self. Following a series of sees Stacy and Robin grew fond of each other. This encouraged her to embark on the uncertain journey of love.

Robin finally got the chance to know Stacy as he had long wished for; her childhood, previous relationship, even how it ended with the loss of her baby. The days coupled to weeks which consequently multiplied to months and their relationship grew.

She appreciated and enjoyed spending time with him. Stacy learnt a lot from her interaction with Robin. He had also gone through quite belligerent life experiences. He grew up under the household of a peasant father who was in a polygamous marriage; his mother was the second out of the four sister wives. At the age of ten, his mother had passed away from a fatal illness, leaving behind, him and his two young sisters, Precious and Primrose. It was each wife's responsibility to fend for her own children. His father could not be of much help as he had a lot of children to support and naturally the most conniving wife would convince him to contribute more to the care of her own children. This left his father with the responsibility of maintaining of order and peace within his family. Lucky to have a roof on top of their heads, being the eldest, Robin had taken up the responsibility to fend for his siblings. He would work to send himself and his siblings to school, get food on the table and get them possible minimal clothing.

The situation worsened when his father passed on. The children from the first wife had grown and were starting their own families so they inconsiderately took for themselves vast of their father's land, leaving Robin and his sisters with barely enough space to cultivate on. Aunty Lucy, his mother's sister came to their aid; she took them to stay with her family. Her husband had not been in total agreement with her, evidenced by how they would constantly engage in arguments regarding their stay. These arguments had not set well with Robin. This led to him engaging his aunt in a discussion to send him and his sisters to a boarding school in the countryside. With it being economically affordable it would be a more accommodating solution. Robin and his sisters would be well kept and Aunt Lucy's marriage would be saved from the series of disagreements.

During the holidays they had seen it better to remain at the school as it was more peaceful. For their accommodation, Robin would pay by carrying out manual jobs around the school premises together with the groundsmen. Despite the burden of responsibilities weighing down on his shoulders, caught off guard, he had fallen in love with Gloria. She was the first woman he got to fall in love with, a daughter of the teacher at his school and she stayed at the teacher's quarters. They had met during the holidays. She was beautiful, gorgeous, kind hearted and well-mannered. She assisted Robin in taking care of his sisters during the holidays as well as the school terms, sourcing for them extra blankets, food and she kept the girls company in his absence.

Robin being bright and intelligent academically, Aunty Lucy was determined to support and give him the best possible education to secure his future. Upon completion of high school she sent him to university. He left his sisters behind at the boarding school. Gloria reassured him that she would keep watch over them in his absence. On vacations he would return to the school and still work there to cover for their accommodation. Driven by his love for Gloria, he had thought to himself that as soon as he found a job after finishing his studies, he would marry her, build a home and have a family with her and stay together with his sisters.

It was during his second year of varsity when he had returned to the boarding school and found Gloria in a critically ill state. Following a tardy diagnosis of scarlet fever she had frequented the hospital. The reason for her frequent admissions had been that the functioning of her organs was deteriorating and her immune system was also slowly shutting down. The state of her health was unpleasant, she was severely compromised. It got worse that the Doctor had to pay her home visits for assessment consultations. Because of this misfortune, Robin had spent little time with her; it was a terrible period for him and his sisters too as Gloria had become part of their little seclusion. A week after his return to University he received a message that Gloria had succumbed to the illness.

Death had claimed the lives of the few people that he had learned to love; Gloria's death caused him great grief. As a result, he became avoidant of getting attached to people fearing the pain of losing them to death. Aunty Lucy's husband then passed on; a tragic car accident claimed his life. He sympathized with his uncle's family for their loss although his uncle's death had not really bothered him because they had an estranged relationship. Aunty Lucy took Robin's sisters back to stay with her. They began spending their holidays there. Robin completed his studies and he moved from Aunty Lucy's to stay independently as a proper bachelor. She refused to permit his sisters and two of her own daughters to do likewise as she insisted that they would only move out if they married. So as they pursued their studies and careers they were stuck with Aunty Lucy.

"Ma! You won't believe who is here," shouted Precious as she stood up from the couch heading towards the door.

Robin had not gone home during the festive season as he usually did because of duty calls. He had been given the assignment to see to the participation of Qadar in the charity projects. However, he had made time towards the end of the first quarter of the year lest Aunty Lucy would get worried.

Upon Robin's entry into the house Precious was surprised and excited, she called Aunty Lucy knowing that she would also be as excited to see him.

Aunty Lucy ran to embrace him. "So just like that, the city swallowed you and you decided to disown us," teased Aunty Lucy as she clasped her sister's huge son into her arms.

"Really disown you, come on now never," Robin responded looking down at Aunty Lucy who was looking up at him with her hands wrapped around his waist.

"It has to be a girl Mama," responded Trish as she entered the living room causing everyone to assemble in laughter. She had come out of her room into the living room eager to see why her mother had been called out and to see the person whose voice she had heard from her room. "Hello brother, "she said, smiling as she continued walking towards him.

"You know, I agree," Aunty Lucy responded letting go of him to allow others a chance to greet him.

With amusement he responded, "Ho! Guys, can we just sit down first."

"See he won't even deny it," Precious responded as she pulled her brother's hand directing him to the couch so he could sit.

"And he is even blushing. Guy, you can't even hide it," Trish responded and again they all laughed.

"Now you two stop. Let my boy be home peacefully, save your interrogations for some other time. Actually, go get busy; go make him some food and prepare his room. Also, these bags are not so heavy."

Trish and Precious giggled continuously as they strolled out of the living room, leaving Aunty Lucy with Robin.

"So come on Rob talk to me; what's the deal with this girl?"

"Honestly Ma, work has been keeping me busy but I was going to make time to come home. Look I'm here."

"I know you got work darling but I can also see that you've got a woman now."

"Where's the rest of the crew?"

"I don't know where they are. Out there I guess, acting grown like you. Nobody tells me anything around here anymore."

"Oh come on Ma don't be like that."

"Am I lying? Like now you are avoiding my question."

"Ma, you are unbelievable but well okay." He sighed deeply. "There really isn't much to tell. It's still early. We're just getting to know each other."

"We're getting somewhere; go on baby."

"There is something peculiar about her. How I feel about her has purged this fear I had regarding falling in love. It happened unexpectedly Ma and she makes me happy."

4 THE ART OF LETTING GO

When the power of love is present, it conquers it all. After 2 years of dating, Stacy and Robin got married. A family! She had to improvise a way so as to allow herself to be prepared to be on the family way. Robin had made it clear to her during their relationship, how much he was expectant to have children of his own. She too would have loved to have children of her own. However, what haunted her were the unending flashbacks of what had happened to her six years ago, the miscarrying and losing of her baby. It was a traumatic experience whose memories she had tried detaching herself from without properly dealing with them. Hence, the incomplete healing of her mental and emotional scar lingered in her innermost being. The idea of starting a family with Robin and having children of her own triggered the flashbacks.

Perhaps if she paid a visit to the places that she last met with Timmy and recall the sequence of events that had transpired leading to them separating, she would be at peace.

"Good morning my love, if you don't wake up at once I'd like to believe you will be running late," said Robin, waking up his wife who appeared reluctant to waking up.

"Good morning to you too. Oh my," she said, yawning. "Don't worry yourself my darling I will not be reporting for work today." She climbed out of bed to help Robin get ready for the day.

Robin looked at her, filled with worry. She rarely missed going to work. "Why? Is there anything troubling you?"

"You are quick to worry, I'm all right. I just feel a little off today so I decided not to go to work. Please may you pass me my gown right there next to you?" As she was getting into her gown she caught him starring hard at her. "Umm and what is that look supposed to mean?"

He refocused his attention on putting on his last stocking and chuckled then lifted his head up. "Well I'm trying to comprehend how such a pretty face as you can fart so much like that."

"I don't fart in my sleep sir," she defended herself then laughed lowly in embarrassment.

"Oh yeah trust me, you sure do, a great deal. One of these days I'll wake you up to confirm the scent I have to endure for a segment of the night."

"Well perhaps those are the perks of being a husband."

They shared a minute of laughter.

"Okay, I have to prepare your food before you run on late; I'm struggling to tie these belts. They seem short or perhaps, I have worn this wrongly."

"Possibly you have put on some weight."

"Not at all." She resumed tying up her garment belts. "Look there we go it fits perfectly well. So, what would you like to have for breakfast?"

"An egg white omelette and a slice of toasted bread will do, thank you."

"That's easy, coming right away," she said hastening out of their bedroom to the kitchen.

Within a few minutes, shorter than the time it would take preparing the requested meal, she returned to the bedroom and abruptly sat on the bed. She threw her back on the bed and with the palm of her left hand covered her forehead.

Walking out of the bathroom Rob found her lying on the bed, "That was quick."

"I couldn't, I just beat the egg into the bowl, and as I was standing, a dizzy spell hit me so I just left it all and came to take a relief."

"Now I'm beginning to worry even more. Are you sure you are okay?"

"No my love you don't have to worry really, trust me. Maybe I just need a little rest that's all."

"Okay if you say so, then I order you to take a strict bedrest for the rest of the day, call me if you will need anything."

Smiling up at her husband, she thought, Robin worried easily; perhaps that was care, although at times Stacy deemed it unnecessary.

"Order noted Doc."

"Good, I will get some breakfast on my way to work and you missy," he reached down for her forehead to stamp a kiss on it, "please take care of yourself".

Later, when Stacy awoke, she felt much better. She took it upon herself to begin her long overdue planned mission. She headed to the park where she would recall everything that transpired towards the termination of her previous relationship, especially, her last conversation with Timmy concerning her pregnancy. On entering the park, she caught sight of the spot they had frequented and at once she remembered how heated and hostile their last conversation had been. An overwhelming feeling came on her as she recalled it all; how she had loved Timmy and how all their dreams and plans at once had crumbled to naught.

The loss of her first love would remain a tormenting scar on her. Would the same apply if she were to bear Robin a baby? Would she constantly be reminded of the loss of her first? At that thought, a sudden gush of emotions overruled her and she burst into tears. Unexpectedly, the dizzy spell hit her again as she was standing. As she tried to reorient herself to the blurry surroundings and allow herself to take a seat, her legs failed her. With the little energy she had she could hardly yell for help.

Timmy had gotten married to Nancy as per their families' arrangement. He had had no choice, as one cannot easily deny their destiny. Out of obligation he had had to comply with his parents' instructions. He had loved Stacy but fighting to be with her was fighting a losing battle. There had been no other way; his parents would have condoned him for marrying her. With each day, he resented himself for leaving her at the most vulnerable state as she was dealing with the loss of her pregnancy.

Though married to Nancy now, the absence of any emotional chemistry between them was evident. It was a marriage of convenience in which, they were obliged to bear children to complete the family's intuition that they were capable of continuing the legacy to the next generation. What propelled the subsistence of their marriage was the web of the inherited wealth and both of them being goal driven. This equipped them duly to bear the responsibility of preserving the legacy for the forthcoming generations. Both of them contributed, it was a give and take setting of mutual concession and compromise.

In the first year of their, marriage they had been blessed with a baby boy, Charlie. Being a father filled Timmy with overwhelming emotions. Guilt struck him; he could not help but think of Cadeau and wished if Charlie could have been his and Stacy's son. Two years after Charlie's birth, Stewart had been born. Despite the severity of emotional detachment between them, they worked hard to be good parents. The family did not communicate much and had aridness of affection within their home. Being financially affable was a way to compensate for parental emotional unavailability.

Nancy knew all about Tim and his first love, Stacy. The thought of having to compete for Timmy's affection with another woman made Nancy to be sceptical of her marriage to him. Their marriage was a race on a thorny plain. Despite that, she was certainly not going to give up easily on their marriage as there was a lot to lose. She had given birth to two healthy legatees to the bequest, let alone, the reputation of her family name. Moreover, it would have seemed an act of disobedience to both their parents' hopes, wishes and desires if she had contradicted the family wishes.

Adhering to the obligations weighed heavy on her. Carrying out the motherly duties to her children by being available for them, managing her office tasks and the least, being a wife to an emotionally and often a physical unavailable husband overwhelmed her. She yearned for Timmy's attention and support which she was now certain she would never receive. After the long wait for him to be more involved in their marriage and be available for his family, years of constant endurance to the harsh and unfavourable living conditions she ran out of patience. She consoled herself by acknowledging how much she had tried and had played her part as she was expected to. She had made up her mind; she was leaving her marriage lest she would drown in depression.

"Father I am saying this to you again, I'm not sure if you are hearing me well when I say I want out of this marriage. I'm not in a happy space and I'm tired of living like this; I can't take it anymore. I'm coming home I thought I should let you and mom know before showing up."

"What do you mean with asking what about the boys?"

As she was on the phone with her father, Timmy walked in to the bedroom.

"I've to go now, I'll call you later to talk about this; thank you, goodbye." She dropped the receiver. She had not discussed her intentions with him so she did not want him hearing them as yet.

Nancy was unaware that before presenting himself

Timmy had been eavesdropping on her conversation long enough.

"Hey Tim, while you take a shower let me go and get your supper ready, "she said as she stormed out of the bedroom escaping the tension that was between them.

5 THE REV'S CALL

As soon as he got back from the boardroom, Rob was informed him that there were a couple of telephone messages received on his behalf. Upon looking at the list of the messages amongst them was one from Reverend Paine. It stood out the most because it was rare of him to call. What could possibly be the matter that he had to call him? He would probably ask Stacy when he got home because the day was almost over. Then he remembered she had not reported for work, he had left her at home. Curious, he sat down to try his luck and call him back.

"Rev, good day; I just got back into the office from a meeting and learnt you were looking for me. What a surprise. Is everything well?"

"Robin! Glad you called me back in time, son. I wish I could say that it is but unfortunately not."

"You are worrying me now father," said Robin in a cracked voice.

"I would like to ask for you to report to St

Emeralds Emergency hospital as soon as possible."

"The hospital!"

"Son, unfortunately I cannot discuss with you the matter at hand in detail over the phone. See you when you arrive."

Immediately Robin stood up, picked up essentials he would need and headed for the hospital. His wife and he had grown fond of Reverend Paine. They both did not have present fathers so he had become the fatherly figure in their lives. Being a significant part of their life, the thought of losing Reverend Paine was not easy for Robin to engage with. The Reverend was in his later life stage but looked fairly healthy. At that thought, he remembered how important it was for Stacy to be alerted too for she was fonder of him than he was.

Unfortunately he couldn't get hold of her as her phone went straight to voicemail, so Robin just left a message.

When he arrived at the hospital, he was surprised when he identified the St Johns Anglican church bakkie in the parking bay. Reverend barely drove it for personal endeavours. Perhaps it was not him after all seeking hospital care. Maybe the caretaker had driven him to the hospital due to the delay the ambulances at times display. His mind raced with thoughts trying to figure out everything as he walked into the hospital.

Upon entering, at the receiving area he saw Reverend Paine from afar talking to someone behind a glass proofed office labelled 'clerk'. With relief he exhaled as he did not appear to be gravely unwell as he had perceived from the sound of urgency in his voice earlier on. Reverend handed over some papers to the hospital clerk. They looked like hospital forms which he submitted with gratitude then concluded the conversation with the clerk and immediately redirected his attention to Robin.

"There you are son, finally! Glad you have made it."

"You bet! How you sounded on the phone almost gave me a heart attack. Could have seen me being driven in here on a stretcher to be admitted just like you."

"Me on a stretcher, admitted, what are you talking about young man?"

"From your call I figured that you might be unwell and needed immediate medical attention."

"Oh no son you read wrongly into this." He reached to hold Robin's shoulder. "It is not me. It's Stacy...." Before he could continue the doctor interrupted them from the casualty ward exit.

"Reverend Paine right," he said as he walked towards them.

"Yes it is I."

"I see from the form you are the next of kin for Ms. Stacy?"

This all did not make sense to the confused poor Robin. His wife was in hospital? How had she ended up here and why was the Reverend the first to be informed yet her husband was unaware? If she had reported for work it would have made sense but she was at home or was supposed to be at home; unless she had stubbornly decided to report for work.

"Oh no, not precisely. I was just standing in. I've contacted the rightful next of kin, her husband, Robin here. Robin, meet the doctor, he received Stacy when she was brought in and is the one who contacted me.

And when I couldn't get hold of you, immediately I came."

Robin feeling a sudden rush of blood giving him heart palpitations and numbness in his legs, tried hard not to give in to the edge of losing control. He sneered and shook the doctor's hand.

"Thank you very much; so kind of you Reverend. Hello doctor, please tell us, how is she doing?"

"Glad to meet you Robin, please don't get worked out. I assure you, she is definitely going to be okay."

Suddenly he felt slight relief, although he could not help wondering what had happened to bring his wife into the hospital for admission. "Oh God, thank you. I'm glad that you reassure us she is going to be okay but excuse me doctor what happened?"

"It was a minor incident. She was found passed out at the park near the jaguar statue by the recreational patron on duty. He reported that he attempted to awaken her up to no avail. Then he realized she was completely unconscious. Immediately, he called for the ambulance and when she arrived with the ambulance—still she was unconscious—on baseline assessment we noted low blood pressure and also blood spots on her dress."

Robin began pacing up and down within width of where the doctor and reverend were standing. With his left hand, he wiped his face from forehead to chin, as if to remove all the agitation he was facing. Then he withdrew to settle on the floor, leaning on the wall he looked at the Reverend with terror. "Blood…from where exactly doc? This is scaring the heck out of me and the more I hear and don't get to actually see her I feel helpless."

Reverend Paine then realized how their conversation was becoming more privately engaged and out of respect of privacy he excused himself to getting a cup of coffee.

"Yes, she was bleeding. Although she was not profusely bleeding we found it necessary to address the bleeding by retaining her blood pressure. We're still yet to run further investigations and figure out what could have possibly caused this; otherwise all her vitals observations are now stable, assuring us that the bleeding is not threatening."

"Okay so for now what is the way forward?"

"We've put her on a drip with Dextrose just to maintain her fluid flow and raise her sugar levels, as she had a low blood sugar level on admission. I suppose she hadn't taken any food. She is receiving oxygen via a face mask too; being in an unconscious state was impairing her breathing but immediately when she regains consciousness it will be removed."

"As long as you are certain she'll be fine doctor. May I please go and see her, perhaps I might feel better."

"Sure you may go ahead, if you perhaps have any questions or need any further clarification there will be a nurse to assist you, please don't hesitate."

"Sure doctor, let me find my way into the ward." At once he stood up and they shook hands.

Robin found his way to where his wife was lying down. Fortunately, she had regained consciousness.

"Goodness Stacy, you gave me a fright."

"Robin!" she exclaimed as she began trying to help herself seat up. "What's going on here?"

"Easy there my love," he said, reaching for her to

help her resume her supine position." How about you just relax a little for now because we sure have a lot of explanation to exchange."

At once she then remembered what had transpired that morning leading her to not going to work. Unfortunately, her memory only managed to recall up to her being at the park. She still wondered what had happened for her to be brought into the hospital for admission. But she would not nag Robin for him to explain because then she would also have to explain why she had decided to leave the house in her unwell state. "Yes Sir, order noted."

"Don't just note orders; you need to start acting on them ma'am," he said, kissing her hand which he was holding in both of his palms.

She looked at him with such admiration and gratitude, delighted by his care, then smiled. "Lesson learnt; now I promise to note and follow your orders."

At that they both chuckled. Subsequently, they were joined by one of the nurses. She entered the room with a smile and greeted them both. She reached for the pillows on Stacy's back, realigned them that she may comfortably lay on them in a semi fowler's position.

"There we go. Are you comfortable," she asked Stacy, who responded with an approval node and a smile.

"I see the mask is off your face," the nurse continued.

"Yeah, I removed it. It was making me feel uncomfortable. And don't worry; I have a self-made doctor here watching me, so trust me to be okay."

They both laughed eyeing Robin who then responded, "Stubborn patient right here I tell you."

"I agree with you there," the nurse said, nodding in agreement with Robin. "Glad to hear that you are feeling okay. I have brought with me the final results of the assessments done. So because of the low sugar levels you came in with Ms. Stacy you had a dizzy spell and fainted. The blood sugar levels as well as your blood pressure have been resolved now by the fluids you got through the drip. We were concerned with the bleeding but can gladly confirm it isn't anything threatening. If anything more I'm happy to congratulate you, the results show that you are in your first trimester, which explains the spotting as it usually occurs when the foetus is implanting into the uterine wall."

"Sorry. What?" responded Stacy in disbelief.

"Yes, you are pregnant my dear. However, I would like to ask you to allow me to arrange for an appointment on your behalf to visit the gynaecology department as this spotting may indicate cervical incompetence and attention needs to be paid to this to ensure the survival of your growing foetus. There may be a need for you to have a cervical cerclage to avoid the occurrence of a miscarriage, depending on the gynae's assessment. Do not be frightened; it's manageable. And please, your body needs rest so allow it to rest more this time around."

The news they had received had caught them unaware. Pleasant as it was, especially for Robin, to Stacy it just rekindled the thoughts of how she had lost her first pregnancy. Robin's excitement reminded her of how Timmy had been excited when she disclosed the pregnancy to him and also how things suddenly changed after she miscarried. She would not be able to live with herself if she went through it again; that was the most tragic experience she had gone through, let alone the pain. She was not sure if she was even ready and prepared for the journey, which she was now to begin. Filled with dread, she looked at Robin who was delighted by the news that he could not even hide his amusement.

6 TO SAVE THE MARRIAGE OR NOT?

Timmy had grown used to having Nancy and the boys around. Watching them as they grew through infancy, adolescence and awaiting adulthood gave him a sense of purpose, that of being a present and a great father to his children. They were his family. Losing Nancy and the boys was not ideal at this moment. It would render null all the effort they had put in for all the years; not to mention how much it would negatively impact their family living separately. Timmy did not wish to entertain the idea of being a father of a broken family, he detested the thought. He knew that despite their unhappiness Nancy had tried to be a remarkable partner in their marriage and an incredible mother to their sons.

Whilst he was stuck on the guilt and self-resentment of letting go off Stacy, he had no idea how much his being emotionally distant was hurting Nancy and their marriage. Nancy had never confronted him; she had concealed all the wrath and emotions and allowed them to pile up. For her it became a norm that she did not find it necessary to discuss or resolve their unsettling marriage. Perhaps she had run out of patience and given up on waiting for him to finally show affection towards her. She had begun to feel defeated. The conversation she had with her father was evident of this.

Timmy felt disappointed in himself. He had not been able to keep the people he loved; those whom he was supposed to love. Had he failed to love? Nancy had left for her parents' house with both their sons. She had not told him about her intentions. She had only informed him that they would be going for the holiday at her parents. Being alone made him realise how lonely and miserable he would become without his family. Even if he was to look for Stacy, would she still be there waiting for him after all the years that had passed? He had to forgive himself for losing Stacy because if he did not—he was going to lose his family too.

Timmy decided he would fight and not lose everything good that had come to him. He chose his family and committed himself to put effort to save his marriage and win his family. The holidays ended without her or his parents summoning him. She returned home with both their sons. Fate had favoured him and now the ball was in his court.

"Wow! The food smells amazing," exclaimed Timmy as he walked into the kitchen.

Smiling, Nancy responded, "Thank you. Well it's still yet to be served, let's hope it tastes likewise."

Nancy always had a welcoming manner, a constant

state of calmness and she never showed resentment towards him; it puzzled Timmy. It seemed as if she was unbothered by the estranged state of their marriage. Although she actually was, little did she know that he knew about her undisclosed mission of separating their union.

He took a chair and helped himself to a seat and interminably glared at her as she continued with preparing the supper. In justification, he consoled himself with the assumption that Stacy had already moved on too with her life. It was more than a decade since their separation. It was possible that she had even forgotten all about him. He was taken out of his thoughts by the sound of cutlery being placed next to his plate as she served him, Charlie and Stewart their supper.

"The food is full of flavour, thank you my dear. But you aren't eating?"

"I've been eating as I was cooking so I'm okay thank you. I've also saved some for myself for later." She noticed how he was different. Very unusual of him; he had returned home in time for supper. He had not fled to isolate himself in the bedroom like a teenage boy as he always did. Not to mention how interactive he was being with her; they hardly sustained general conversations besides greeting each other or discussing work progress and the wellbeing of their sons.

As she was busy with tidying up the kitchen her heart delighted at the conversations they were having and the laughter she heard in her background of him and the boys. For a moment she felt satisfied. This was the family she had always yearned for, a happy family with both parents actively involved and present.

"Thanks mom, the food was amazing—see we all did justice to your cooking—everyone cleared their plates," Stewart said as he took the empty plates to the kitchen sink.

"Impressing! Perhaps you wouldn't mind seconds?"

"No ways—thank you."

They both broke into laughter. Stewart had grown to be the joker and the most interactive of the two boys. Moreover, he was more close to his mother. Charlie was closer to Timmy. Timmy would take Charlie with him to work so Charlie could be oriented to the running of the business. He was growing up and she rested assured that at some point he was also going to be involved in ensuring the successful running of the company.

"Stewart and I are going to see a basketball game at the community court down the street."

"No way! This late and what time are you guys coming back?"

"Come on mom; we are not going to sleep there." Charlie always took the initiative of telling their mother when they would go out. He was more of the adult; responsible enough to watch over himself and Stewart.

"It's okay my dear, let them go. We could do with some privacy in here for a while."

"Oh wow dad, are we crowding your space that much?"

"Just be conscious of the time Charlie; we don't want your mother worrying about you guys all night and you know you ought to be responsible right?"

"Sure cool, enjoy the privacy," he said, heading towards the door quickly before Nancy had anything to say and delay them.

Stewart followed and on his way out he patted his father's shoulder, gave a hug to his mother who was standing by the door and left.

"Okay, suppose that's my cue. Do you perhaps need anything else before I retire to bed," Nancy asked, prepared to leave.

"Actually, yes, please, before you go may you seat with me?"

"Sorry, I cannot. I'm really exhausted. It's been a long day for me and tomorrow I've an early morning so I really need all the rest I can get. Goodnight," Nancy responded as she left the room. Again, how unusual of Timmy. However, she had suppressed her pain of being in this unhappy marriage for too long and she was not going to allow his short act to manipulate her into thinking otherwise. She had made her decision; she was divorcing him. The boys had grown up enough to be able to decide whom they would want to stay with.

Passing through Stewart's bedroom she decided to take a nap in there as she waited for them to return. She would wake up on his return and go to her bedroom or rather not. She would rather share the bed with her son. Seventeen years old, Stewart detested sharing his bed but she would rather have to deal with her son than her strange husband.

Not only did she avoid Timmy that night, a couple of weeks passed and she continued to share Stewart's bed. Whenever he would ask her why she was sleeping in his room she would use a silly excuse that she had unexpectedly passed out.

One morning, some hours before dawn, Timmy got

the courage to confront his wife. "Nancy, come on wake up."

"Ey, not so loud you'll wake up Stewart. Is it morning already?"

"Just a little early into it, it's way after two."

"Oh great—at least there is still some more time to sleep. So what's going on why are you waking me up?"

"Nancy this is not your room and listen—it's cold alone there in that bed without you."

"Are you being for real right now Tim? You came here to wake me up for you to just say that?"

"Yes and to plead with you to please come to bed. It's cold and lonely being alone and listen, I miss you."

"Are you kidding me? You got to be, really, because Timothy all these years of us being together you hardly notice my presence, let alone my recent absence. Come on who are you trying to play here?"

"Okay, can we not do this here? We'll wake up the boys."

"How about we don't even do this, here or anyway, because I honestly don't have the energy."

"Whatever the problem is, it's been going on for too long. We can't keep avoiding it and going on like everything is okay."

"Fine, but of all times it had to be now? This is honestly ridiculous," Nancy whispered angrily as she led the way to their bedroom.

Timmy was left behind peeping into each bedroom to see if the boys had not woken up, then he followed her.

The light was off—she hesitated switching it on and decided to leave it off. However, on attempting to take a seat on the edge of the bed, she missed and fell on the mat. When Timmy entered, he switched on the light; to his surprise Nancy was picking herself up.

After a chuckle, he said, "Oh! So now you sleep walk?"

"My rods are clearly failing me, perks of aging I guess."

"Hahahaha," he said sarcastically. "You need to work on your joking skills; will get Stewart to help on that."

"Okay. I hope you didn't come to wake me up and bring me here so just you could mock me."

"Not at all; pardon me. But of course I disagree with you aging; you don't seem to be aging at all. In my eyes, you are getting younger. The more I'm getting old, the more I'm getting to see how much of a beautiful and wonderful lady you are."

"Are we okay over here," said Nancy laughing at Timmy. She raised the back of her hand and reached for his forehead as if to assess his temperature and she continued, "You are sure we are not some sort of sick?"

He took her hand off his forehead and pulled it down with him as he knelt down on one knee.

"I'm serious my love."

"Okay now this isn't funny. Should I be worried? What is going on here and what are you doing?"

"Shhh, may I please ask you to allow me to do the talking? I know I haven't done justice to you in this marriage. I haven't been the best husband to you and I really feel bad for that because you have been nothing short of being an incredible woman to me; a wholehearted mother and an amazing wife. I would like to apologize for all the emotional pain that I might have put you through…" Timmy couldn't help the tears that were strolling down his cheeks as he spoke to his wife.

In all the years of their marriage this was the first instance of maintaining eye contact with him for that long. Hearing him acknowledge exactly how she felt and taking full responsibility of it struck her. The measure of genuineness in his apology, spoken by his tears caused Nancy to break into tears too.

"…despite that we didn't start up this marriage well, you had hope that it'd eventually work out and even against all odds you still didn't give up on us. Nancy, I'm deeply humbled by the care you've shown and once again I'd like to apologize for being an unfair partner to you. Please forgive me my love. I would like for us to work on our marriage. May you allow us a chance so that I can make it right by you?"

An apology was the least she had expected from him. To think she was ready to walk out of their marriage! She had given up. The long awaited turnaround had seemed so unreachable. Kneeling down to him, sobbing, she held his cheeks, each with each of her palms.

"You have no idea of the weight you've lifted off my shoulders, by just saying these words Timothy. Thank you."

7 HAPPY ANNIVERSARY!!

Stacy was uncertain of being pregnant as she feared how derailed she would be if anything would happen to the pregnancy. She did not want to experience again the horrors she went through with her first pregnancy. As if knowing she was pregnant and needed medical attention to keep the pregnancy safe was not overwhelming enough for her, a few months in gestation, Stacy's midwife confirmed with her on follow-up assessments that her womb was carrying two foetuses. Stacy got medical attention and successfully carried her pregnancy to term. She gave birth to two beautiful girls. Holding them in her hands and seeing how attached her husband was to his daughters from the first time of setting his eyes on them she felt different, grateful. They were blessed.

Their daughters grew well and quite remarkably. Nevertheless, every time she saw them as they grew she could not help but wonder about Cadeau, what would he have grown up to become. Timothy had left her to deal with all the grief and pain all alone as he went and got married as his family had arranged for him. He had probably moved on with his life and had forgotten about the loss of Cadeau by replacing him with another. Fortunate for him to be able to move on quickly whereas it had taken her a while to do so. It had been more than twenty years after the miscarriage but the loss never felt less raw.

Robin, her ordained life partner, who was an amazing husband and father to their children, had come her way when she had least expected that she could ever be capable of loving anyone again. In their twenty years of marriage, Stacy was contented with her family; she rendered herself favoured.

"So mommy, I have got something to tell you but you ought to keep it a secret okay," said Sheila to her mother.

"A secret, that sounds interesting, please do tell."

Whispering to her mother's ear, "Please go to your room in the meantime and only come back for dinner at around half past sixish together with daddy and please be dressed in formal."

"Okay…."

"Yep."

"So that's all?"

"Yes mommy"

"Sheila honey that's no secret, you could have simply said that out loud."

"Well actually mom, secrets too have stages of being told so take this as the first and to make it interesting if you want to know the juicy part of the rest of the secret please do follow each of the stages I'm to instruct you."

Just as Sheila and Stacy were in the midst of their conversation, Shalom stomped in.

"Hey mom and Sheila the way you guys look, so serious, what are you on about? If it's about me, I'm sorry I'm late. Couldn't help it my classes took forever to finish today."

"Calm down, it's not even about you. In fact, not everything is about you," Sheila said.

"Wow, so harsh Why are you so grumpy? Okay! So! Is it some boy trouble? Going to mommy for some consolation? Trust me been there and mommy knows best." Shalom rolled her eyes as she paced into the living room.

"Okay both of you need to just calm down and stop with whatever this is, be nice to each other okay and hello to you too Shalom."

"Anyway, I was just telling mom about our little surprise that we have for her."

"Oh yes! My bad, it totally skipped my mind. Thank you for remembering Sheey."

"Okay so both of you, are you just going to shut me out like that," Stacy said.

Sheila smiled at her sister. "Like, she is being stubborn she won't do what I asked her to do. I've been asking her to go to her bedroom join her lovely husband, chill and come back when dinner is ready."

Shalom turned to look at her mother. "Come on mom it's not a big deal we just want to do a little surprise for you and Dad; so yeah please help yourself and go relax then refresh and come back for the evening meal."

Stacy raised her hands in surrender. "Okay, fine, seems I don't have a choice as you are ganging up all on me."

Robin was busy reading from a newspaper when she got into the bedroom. Everyone seemed to be occupied and only she was left idle. Stacy then decided to interrupt her husband.

"You returned from work early today, I guess it's one of the lucky days."

"Yeah, typical of Fridays."

"Makes sense."

"So what's new in the current affairs?"

Stacy did not have much interest with current affairs and she would rather be with the girls or in the kitchen than engage in a conversation with him regarding news. For her to be sitting with him discussing current affairs was unforeseen. Puzzled by her sudden interest in news, he closed the paper, placed it aside and took a good glare at his wife.

"What! Why are you looking at me like that? I was just asking it wouldn't hurt to know a little."

"Someone is bored, what's going on?"

"Okay fine, confirmed, I'm bored. I'm all alone with nothing to do. You are absorbed into the news and the girls sent me off, so I don't know what to do with myself?"

"Sent you off? I don't understand, what do you mean?"

"They asked me to leave, come here and relax. I actually don't know what exactly I'm supposed to be doing to relax and yeah refresh. Then you and I should present ourselves in formal, yeah, for dinner." She let out a laugh.

"Not that any of this makes sense but I surely wouldn't mind. It actually gives me some time to spend with you. Come closer, come seat right here next to me and I'll show you how to relax."

"I won't lie. I'm really curious to know what they are up to. I mean are you not?"

He looked and gave her a charming grin. "So much drama in this house, I'm not going to comment." He reached for his newspaper.

He did not respond to her question and she continued, standing up. "Maybe I should just tiptoe and peep on them."

Pulling her to the bed, "Nope…You'll do no such thing. Come on let the kids be."

"What must I do then in the meantime?"

"I don't know sweetheart figure yourself out maybe, sleep or you could take a shower and start preparing; 6 is just now."

She went off, leaving Robin who then submerged himself deep into thought. He reflected on his journey of building a family and fatherhood. After the minor mishap at the park that had resulted in them becoming aware that Stacy was on the family way and knowing how she had lost her first pregnancy caused them to worry about a recurrence. It had been a challenging time for them both. His family and Stacy's had offered them the utmost support. Rev Paine too had been a constant source of morale support. He had encouraged them spiritually and prayed with them. Seeing the girls incited him of how satisfied he was to be a family man. He vowed to himself that he would take it upon himself to ensure that the same sentiment of satisfaction, peace and happiness was enjoyed by them all within his household.

When Stacy was done she went back to join her

husband who seemed to be deep in thought. As he noticed her entry he instantaneously began a conversation with her.

"I've just been thinking and reflecting on how much we have thrived together making the responsibility of having a beautiful family bearable. I appreciate you."

"Thank you for the kind words my love and I'd have never asked for a better husband than you, it's really quite fascinating looking at how time flies."

"At times it feels like we just met then again I'm reminded by taking a look at how the girls have grown how time glides on."

"But it's been crazy, can you imagine how our lives underwent a series of spontaneous plot twists. Pain, sorrow, happiness and love; all that has brought us to where we are."

"Indeed such is life my darling, different situations one ought to face but they too will pass. —Look at us we have survived."

Their conversation was disrupted by a knock. It was Shalom informing them that they were left with a few minutes to prepare and join them. Robin had not refreshed so he hurriedly did and in no time they were both dressed in formal as instructed. As they walked into the living room they were startled by a squad of voices which yelled "SURPRISE" at once.

The room was filled; indeed, it was a surprise. Stacy's mother, Stacy's sister together with her husband who held their son in his arms, Aunty Lucy, Robin's sisters and their respective families were in the living room. Rev Paine and the girls, Shalom and Sheila, stood behind everyone holding up a banner which read, 'Happy Anniversary!' It was astounding. In the twenty years of their marriage, they had not had a big celebration of their wedding anniversary but their two magnificent daughters had organized one for them.

"Wow I'm out of words, these girls!!...," Stacy said. She could hardly speak as she was overwhelmed with emotions of being thought of in this manner and to such an extent. Robin, who stood by Stacy, grasped her hand to strengthen her. In response to his gesture, they exchanged smiles and then she continued, "You've really outdone yourselves girls. Thank you for all this…the effort and wow everyone here you have no idea how much we appreciate you taking your time."

Before Robin could say anything Aunty Lucy impeded him and faced everyone as she pointed to where the food was, "Can we go to the table and all help ourselves before the food gets cold; we might as well talk all we want through the meal."

It was a sensible suggestion so everyone willingly followed her lead and in no time the room broke into a roar of conversations. Being surrounded by people who had been constantly around and supportive of them gave positive reinforcement. To add to that was their shared feeling of achievement and satisfaction at celebrating twenty years of marriage. Most importantly was the gratitude that Stacy and Robin felt and later disclosed to their guests who had done a lot for them over the years.

8 WHAT IS GOING ON WITH SHEILA?

As the years passed, Stacy had learned to be at peace and grateful of Timmy's absence. If he had been present, her life would not have turned out as pleasant as it was now. As her daughters grew, just like any mother, Stacy hoped that they would not have to suffer heartbreak. The thought of how difficult it had been for her to deal with losing love, she would do anything to avert Shalom and Sheila from going through a similar experience. As much as some life experiences are inevitable, she would try to protect them. Each of the girls grew into her own peculiar personality, Sheila was more of reserved and quite intelligent and Shalom was more technical. She too was intelligent but not as analytical as Sheila was; her strength lay in hands-on skills.

After completing their secondary education, the talk in the house was now centred on proceeding to tertiary education. Surprisingly, only Shalom had keenly engaged in the conversation. Sheila was often the most enthusiastic with matters that concerned her academics and yet she had not voiced out much about her intentions. Stacy and Robin began to assume that she was undecided given the broad range of choices she could make. She had excelled in all her subjects. After asking her if by chance she needed assistance with making a choice and she refused, they decided to allow her to take her time. Time passed, and they attempted to ask her again. She would give the excuse that she was busy with researching and compiling the unnamed career program she wanted to pursue and the institution of choice.

Sheila could not keep it to herself any longer. She had to tell her mother what was troubling her because she was growing exceedingly uncomfortable. Avoiding her family would not do any help. The thought kept her up, wondering how she would make known her case. She wanted to go ahead and proceed with her academics but she was not in the right space to do so. This she knew would crush her parents with the high hopes they had for both her and Shalom. At dawn she went to the kitchen to get a snack. Whilst she was at it she decided to prepare breakfast.

Shalom then joined her; she was the least of her favourite company as she would not stop inciting questions about her plan to pursue her studies. She would begin talking about it in their parents' presence brewing up the discussion turning heads to her inquisitively. She wasn't to blame; it was an exciting venture for her which she was eager to start on. Alas, she didn't understand that they did not share the same view.

"Hey Sheey."

"Morning Shalom."

"Pardon my observances but you don't seem to look well, are you okay?"

"I'm okay just couldn't get enough sleep."

"Oh okay I see. Thought you were upset after yesterday's conversation regarding next fall and school."

"Actually about that, I'd appreciate it if you would just ease up a little Shalom. I am not as excited about it as you are. Whenever you bring it up it just makes me so uncomfortable. Better you talk about your intentions in my absence."

"I don't understand Sheila, what is the problem really? I just don't understand cause it's not even a big deal really for you. After all you apparently are the intellectually gifted. It's just a matter of choosing."

"Spot on you don't understand so how about just not talk about it in my presence and not put me under so much pressure. I really don't need the attention let alone pressure."

As they were in the midst of their conflict, Stacy walked in. When they noticed her presence they both suddenly went quiet. She did not want to seem like an intruder in matters that did not concern her. Her daughters were adults enough to decide whether they needed her to intervene or not. It was up to them to approach her. After they had exchanged morning greetings they sat down to have breakfast.

It was evident that there was tension in the room. Stacy was curiously wondering what could have blown up such an aggressive conversation between them but remembering that she had to give them the responsibility to handle their own conflicts, she silently continued eating.

Unsettled by the present tension around them, Sheila felt it was probably better to just feel bad all at once by using this awkward moment to talk to her mother and let her know the reason why she was slacking on the matters regarding her academic progression. Challenging as it seemed, it had to be done and better off without her father's presence. "Mom there is something I would like to discuss with you."

"I guess that's my cue. May I please be excused," Shalom said, getting ready to stand.

"No please don't go just yet," Sheila said, reaching to hold her sister's hand. "Sit. I need to say this in the presence of both of you and of course dad will know later."

"Sure go ahead my darling you may speak, your father will join us soon," Stacy said.

"I can't go to school next fall. I'm sorry to say this. I know how disappointing it is for you to hear this from me and I have been meaning to let you know. But there is no easy way to say this. Mommy I'm on the family way."

Tongue stuck, unaware of how to respond to the news, Stacy was filled with so many questions to ask her daughter but she did not know what the questions were. Finally, she settled on, how could her daughter have kept such an important issue from her? She thought she had created an environment conducive enough for her daughters to discuss anything with her. Yet, even this could not come out of her mouth.

Sheila had lowered her head, expecting her mother to say something. The silence was making her anxious.

She was prepared to handle however her mother responded; get angry at her, ask her all the questions she needed to know regarding her state, anything, she just wanted to hear how her mother had received the news. Shalom also was silent. Sheila looked up at her sister.

Shalom had already started a dispute earlier with her sister, she didn't want to worsen the situation by saying anything which would offend or upset Sheila. She looked anxiously from her mother to her sister and then lowered her head to wait for them to speak.

Robin then entered. As he walked towards his chair, it seemed no one had noticed his presence. To add to that the room was unusually quiet. As he pulled out his chair to sit, he looked at his wife who looked distraught and at the edge of breaking down. He crossed over his eyes to Sheila who could barely hold her head up then to Shalom who seemed uncomfortably distant.

Sheila already drenched in guilt could not stomach telling her father. Seeing how disappointed her mother was unsettled her enough.

Shalom felt stuck to her chair, not sure if she was even supposed to be around. The matter seemed beyond her. Sheila had involved her in an awkward and very uncomfortable situation. She looked at her mother to see if her mother would take the lead and begin a conversation.

The silence was unbearable especially for Robin who was clueless on what the matter was. Poor Stacy, keeping the sobs internal, did not manage to keep the tears from falling on her cheeks letting go all the emotions and anguish building up within. She looked up and saw Robin and Shalom glancing at her. She could not bear it. She stood up and left, heading for her bedroom. Robin followed her.

Sheila broke into tears. The fact that she was responsible for what was happening overwhelmed her.

Shalom filled with sympathy for her sister reached for her and held her hand.

9 THE WARMTH OF A MOTHER'S LOVE

Sheila's disclosure of her pregnancy not only disappointed Stacy but it triggered the reopening of her own closed wound. She was just a year older than Sheila and in college when she had also fallen pregnant. She had been willing to drop everything to be a mother to her precious to-be born baby and also be the wife to the man she loved. Only after a few months had she lost them both; the two people who were close to her heart. In addition to that, how challenging it had been for her to get back on her feet.

After she had shared with Robin the shocking news, surprisingly, he had taken no time to come to terms with it and had advised her to engage in a conversation with Sheila. Many constant questions were ringing in her head. Who was responsible for the baby her daughter was caring? Was he going to accept the responsibility to support Sheey and the baby? Did he love her daughter? Was he a good man capable of being a commendable father as well as husband? Were he and her daughter ready to become parents? How old was he even and if he was young, what would become of both their academics and pursuit of their careers? There was even more to these questions but perpetually wondering and scrutinizing on her own was not going to give her the right answers. Perhaps it was time for her to sit down and have a mutual exclusive conversation with her daughter.

When she had fallen pregnant with her son, she hardly knew anything about being pregnant. Delaying the revealing of her pregnancy, had been, she believed, the reason she miscarried. Perhaps if she had disclosed it to her mother or sisters they would have talked to her on how to care for herself as well as the pregnancy and prevent or reduce the chances of losing the pregnancy. Timmy had been there to support her and his involvement had been incredible but he too had never witnessed the care of or taken care of a pregnant woman. It had really been brave of Sheila to disclose to her family that she was pregnant and perhaps her disclosure was a cry for help and consolidation.

Sheila needed to know that her family were going to be there for her. Indeed, she was in need and would really appreciate their support, care and guidance more than ever. She was in an undoubtedly overwhelming situation which if handled alone could possibly buoy up a disastrous outcome.

Shalom was alone in the sitting room when her mother entered in a colourful and floral dress.

"Wow mom, wow you look amazing. What's the occasion?"

"Thank you my darling, spring is the occasion. I had to look for a dress which would blend in with the season."

"Well! Spot on mom."

"I see you're sitting here alone. Any idea where your sister could be?"

"She should be in her room. These past few weeks she barely spends time out of her room. I understand she might be feeling unsettled with this whole issue, so perhaps she's a bit avoidant especially of you and dad."

"I know and I understand, "responded Stacy as she walked to sit next to Shalom with a warm reassuring look. She continued, "Frankly this is not what I wanted for her, let alone expected from both of you. But well no one is perfect we're all susceptible to making mistakes and this is hers. I don't want her to be held back by this situation. There is more ahead waiting for her". Reaching for her daughter's chin, her eyes flooding with tears Stacy looked at Shalom and continued, "I want to be there for you, you're my baby girls. You should never have to deal with anything alone. It saddens me that our relationship has grown alienated; I can hardly have a conversation with your sister now."

She had never seen her mother in such a distraught state, she looked defeated. Unaware of how to comfort her mother or how to best respond Shalom responded. "I hear you mom, I'm happy to hear you want to reach out to her; I was wondering how long it would take you because father has been checking on her. We love you mommy and I'm sure Sheey feels terrible for disappointing you and hurting. It will be easier if you go to her, she really needs you," Shalom said, wiping the tears running on her mother's cheeks.

With a smile, feeling lightened Stacy responded,

"Such sound advice from my own daughter. How did you both grow up all of a sudden? I wasn't ready yet but oh well whether grown up or young don't you forget I'm still your mother okay." Stacy winked at her daughter and she stood up.

"Love you mom."

"Bye; let me go and check on your sister."

Unaware of how to begin the conversation after Sheila had opened the door for her, Stacy went into the room with a smile, a gesture to show that she was coming in peace. Stacy sat on the stool by the study desk which, was positioned close to the window to allow Sheila to take a break by glancing outside. The passing cars perhaps and birds were a nice distraction whenever she would get bored of studying. Stacy got distracted watching the bright flowers falling off the trees as the spring breeze stroked them. Smiling, she turned to her daughter who seemed uncomfortable being in the same room with her. Not sure if she had the appropriate choice of words, Stacy began, "The view is really alluring during this season."

"I agree. Most of the times I wouldn't even study. I'd be caught up with the sight of the beautiful nature."

"So how are you doing?"

"I'm okay and honestly, I'm relived at the same time surprised to have you coming in here. I had come to terms with knowing that you could not stand the sight of me. I understand and I'm really sorry mom."

These words struck deep into her. Her own daughter thought her mother could not stand the sight of her. So she was on the run in her own home, the supposed primary space for safety, comfort and security. Stacy felt disappointed in herself. "I feel disappointed in myself too. I feel I have failed to be the mother that I'm supposed to be to you."

"That's not true mommy. You're an amazing mother."

Hearing her daughter reassure her put her at ease. "Please give mommy a hug," she said extending her arms.

After releasing her, Sheila returned to seat on her bed.

"If anything honey I should've been coming to check up on you. I'm quite disappointed in myself and I'm sorry my baby. I feel from my side it was absolutely duty negligence." She dragged her stool close to where Sheila was sitting and held her hand and with the other hand she lifted her daughter's chin so she could look directly at her face. "I'm really sorry my baby but mommy is here now for her little girl. Okay?"

Her mother apologizing to her for being put in a situation that she had caused made Sheila feel helpless. She had not intended to put her mother in such a situation of doubting herself. Her mother had been nothing short of being the most amazing mother any girl could ask for. She could not hold back the tears, so she let them fall on her chicks. "No mom. You don't have to feel that way. You have been the best; I wonder if I'll become at least half the mom you are."

Flattered, Stacy smiled. "You don't have to worry about that; the nurturing gift comes naturally. You'll be surprised that you might even grow into a better mother than I."

"Thank you mama, you've no idea how much you just being here and saying all the right words means to me," Sheila said as they both wiped off the tears that had fallen on their faces.

"Pleasure is mine Sheila. Besides the uneasy thoughts of becoming a new mother, how are you doing?"

"I'm okay thank you. There isn't much to tell except how terrible the nausea has been, especially if I have anything with lactose."

"Oh I hear you. I didn't have those but I heard how terrible it can be. I'm sorry honey but you'll survive it. So apparently it gets better after the sixteenth week of pregnancy."

"Wow, then I'm still going to endure this for a long while, to be precise say about two more weeks."

"If I'm hearing you well, are you telling me you are 14 weeks far?"

"Yes mama, I'm in my second trimester and I feel the days seem to be moving by so quickly."

"Wow, so far. Baby I can't believe you kept this secret for so long."

"I wanted to tell you sooner than I did mama but it was hard for me to do so. I hated the thought of disappointing you and dad," she answered with embarrassment, fiddling with her pillow which she had put on her thighs.

As she sat with her arms folded looking straight at her daughter she felt pity. "Trust me I can relate to that. I did the same too with my first pregnancy but we'll not talk about it. We have to focus on you. So may I ask you what I believe is a very sensitive question. Who is the father to the baby and are you guys okay?" Stacy hoped that the answer to her question would be pleasant. She could not help to imagine her daughter being faced with a challenging situation similar to the one that she had been in with her first pregnancy. She took a long sincere stare at her daughter to make sure that she would not miss any form of non-verbal expressions in response.

For a moment, Sheila acted as if her mother was not there. She smiled, looking down at her belly, rubbing across it with the palm of her left hand. Then she seemed to remember that her mother had asked her a question and was waiting for her to answer.

"Yes we are fine. He knows about the pregnancy and he is excited about it. He is a great guy mama and he has been very supportive through this whole time."

So she had been getting support from someone else. A rush of jealousy filled Stacy. Her due diligence was being taken over by another. She was supposed to be her daughter's main confidant, the first person to know anything going on with her child whether unpleasant or pleasant. However, she was relieved that Sheila seemed so sure of her partner. It was a good thing that he was responsible enough to be involved and also make her happy. "You seem so sure; I'm relieved that you're both okay with this. I want you to be loved and be happy. So tell mommy more about this mystery guy." Their conversation was going on pretty well. Her daughter was settled as she talked to her mother.

Blushing, Sheila continued, "His name is Charlie and he is twenty-four years old. He is quite a charmer and very much a gentleman. So we've been dating for say—three years. I met him at the city library. So he was giving away school books which he was done using and needed to get rid of. Ms. Shaw the librarian then asked for me to assist her and I did. As I packed the books I saw one for bookkeeping which, I had been long looking. So I was excited, I couldn't contain the excitement and I jumped. Then he noticed I guess and he said to Ms. Shaw I could own it. He then offered to give me tutorials in the subject. So yeah, we would meet here and there. He'd tutor me then we became friends. Yeah and then and then this."

"Interesting that's quite interesting really. Look at you. She can't even hide the excitement on her face from only talking about him. Okay honey, so we need to discuss the way forward. When are we going to meet the man? I honestly think it's only fair that we also get to meet him and I'm sure his parents are eager to see you too?"

That was an unexpected request. Stunned she responded, "About that mom, I just don't know. Well, I thought perhaps we should wait for them to invite us over."

"But honey there isn't much time. We can't keep waiting. What if they make us wait forever. I'll let you and Charlie discuss and be the frontrunners in this situation but I'll give you a restricted time frame to get it all sorted." She was ready to defend her child, to avoid Sheila being faced with the predicament that she had faced. Stacy wanted to protect her child from any disappointment. The sooner the involvement of her daughter's partner and his family in addressing the matter the better. With firmness she continued, "Two weeks should suffice as I'll also be using that time to talk to your dad and discuss this situation."

Robin was against Stacy's suggestion of inviting Charlie and his family to their house. He thought they should be invited by Charlie's family instead. However,

Stacy seemed quite adamant about her suggestion. She then got support from Aunty Lucy who agreed with her that the matter needed to be discussed and resolved as soon as possible. They needed to see him, know the kind of person he was, his intentions regarding Sheila and the unborn baby and also see if he was even capable of taking the responsibility of having a family.

10 A BOLT FROM THE BLUE

After his announcement to his family that he was responsible for making a girl pregnant there was a big rift in the house. He loved Sheey unquestionably; he wanted to be there for her and their child. Against all odds, he was willing to do anything to marry her.

When they had last discussed the issue he had acknowledged and apologized to his parents for not doing things the right and appropriate way. He had also emphasized to them his intentions to marry her with or without their support. He had even made it clear that if they wished to disown him or strip him off all the privileges due to him, he was not going to change his mind.

The request for him to visit Sheila's home put Charlie in a state of despair. And now once more he had to face the dilemma of discussing with them concerning the way forward. They would not support him, that, he knew for a fact. The good thing is that Sheila had told him that her mother had offered to extend an invite to them instead. They both agreed that it would work better that way. He was going to inform his parents about the invite. Their decision to honour it or not would spell out their final decision regarding their support of him starting a new life as an independent family man.

Charlie valued his parents' support, care and input into his life and most importantly their knowledgeable advice. However, he could not help query their instant objection of his relationship with Sheila even though they did not know her. He prepared himself by anticipating an unfavourable response from them regarding the invitation.

Stewart was the only one supporting him in the situation. Perhaps Stewart could mediate for him by explaining to his parents how important it was for him to have their support. Stewart also bore the responsibility of informing them that they had been invited to come over to the girl's house by her parents to discuss the way forward regarding the matter. Stewart was successful in convincing their parents to support his brother; they accepted the invite.

Timmy called Charlie. As they were engaging in a discussion he vented how disappointed he was in Charlie for not being responsible and not holding high the family name through having a child out of wedlock. In addition, Charlie had disrespectfully addressed the issue to them, threatening to exclude himself from the family if they were not willing to come on board with him.

Despite verbally reprimanding his son, Timmy was impressed with his son's courage and determination in fighting for his love. It reminded him of what he had failed to do and as a result had paid for by living a good part of his life in misery, guilt and regret. He did not want the same to happen to his son. When he had been in a similar situation with Stacy, he had wished that the protocols would have been changed. Unfortunately, it had not happened as he had wished. Now he had the authority to correct and change things for the benefit and advantage of his son. He had to do right by Charlie, something his parents had failed to do by him.

Nancy had exhausted all her objections regarding her son's marital intentions. As much as she was disappointed, she was glad that he had found someone he loved of his own accord. He was not compelled to getting into an arranged relationship; she knew how disastrous it could be.

As scheduled, the day came for Timmy's family to pay a visit to Sheila's family.

Sheila was excited to see Charlie's family. On the other hand, he was quite nervous.

Stacy, Aunty Lucy and the twins prepared above and beyond to receive their visitors. Sheila already had her bags packed, ready to leave whenever they were given the blessings by their parents. Aunty Lucy had agreed to accompany Sheila to her new home. Sheila would settle in easier with aunt's help.

The table was set and ready when they arrived. Everyone stood to one side of the table with eyes glazed to the door as Robin went to open and welcome their long awaited guests. Beautiful and classy Nancy was the first to enter. On seeing her, Stacy could not help but admire her appearance and how she carried herself. Nancy was followed by a tall, handsome young man. Upon entering he gazed at Sheila and passed a laze smile. It was obvious that he was Charlie. Charlie proceeded to greet Robin and hand over a bottle of wine. Upon receiving the bottle of wine, Robin called for his wife to come and help attend to their guests. On her way, she and Nancy exchanged greetings then she extended her greetings to Charlie. Afterwards, she gestured them to the living room. She led as they followed. Aunty Lucy, Sheila and Shalom followed behind their guests.

Nancy was delighted by how welcoming Stacy was, how she talked to them and everyone in the room. She was amazed with her gentle, spirited, cheerful, simple and soft spoken character. When Stacy excused herself to go and put the wine in the kitchen, Nancy followed her and offered to give her a hand. Stacy accepted her kind gesture by smiling and nodding in approval. She appreciated an extra hand because it seemed that the other ladies had gotten carried away by the young man.

"Thank you for offering to help; there isn't much left to do really."

"That's fine don't mention. It's the least I can do."

"Okay so I'll put this here and then we can take the bowls to the dining table."

"It's okay I'll just follow your lead."

"Sure, that'll be okay."

The conversation continued as they arranged the bowls into trays. Sheila had mentioned that Charlie still had both parents. Stacy was puzzled by the absence of Nancy's husband. Perhaps he was busy or maybe he disapproved of the relationship. She was curious of his absence and wanted to ask her in a non-offensive manner as she treasured the friendship that they had shortly established.

"So Nancy, Sheila had informed us that Charlie was going to come with his parents and brother. I'm wondering why you came with Charlie alone?"

"Oh yeah indeed that's true. Thank you for asking. Pardon me; I got carried away and forgot to inform you."

"It's okay."

"My husband being such a gentleman decided on our way to get a bouquet of flowers. And because we were running out of time we just decided that Charlie and I should come so that we would not keep you waiting for long."

"Oh I see but they didn't have to put themselves through such trouble."

"Difficult to convince someone whose mind is already made up."

"I know right. I can so imagine but truly your husband is such a gentleman."

"He is hey; he really is, I won't lie, I'm really honoured to be his wife."

"That's sweet, I'm glad we have mutual feelings towards our husbands. Robin came into my life when I least expected and he filled quite a void that I had been living with. I'm so glad Sheila will be able to get support on this journey from both of us."

They took the bowls of food to the table. The conversations were flowing merrily. It was amazing how Charlie and his mother easily fit into Sheila's family. On taking the last set of bowls from the kitchen to the dining table they both noticed flowers placed on the wooden stool close to the entrance to the dining room. Stacy then commented, "That should show the arrival of the other guys. Seems they've been escorted by Robin. He's the one who never knows what to do or where to put flowers."

They both laughed and Nancy responded, "Can never blame him—glad they didn't take too much time."

"True, they are just on time to dig in. Let's proceed. I'll come and put the flowers into a vase with water."

When they entered the dining room, everyone was intertwined in the conversation web. Stacy's eyes were deceiving her. It was not possible; she could not believe it. Perhaps she was hallucinating. As they placed food on the side rails she kept looking at him to be sure of what she was seeing. Indeed, it was him in the flesh, in her house. His smile and voice still the same, although he looked a bit aged. He had advanced in years. My Timmy, she thought to herself and then her thought was interrupted by Nancy's voice.

"Thank you my love for the flowers. Stacy meet my husband Timmy and our last boy Stewart. I'm sure you've already made yourself known to the rest," she smiled, looking at Charlie for confirmation and then continued, "And this remarkable and kind woman who has been very warm and welcoming is Stacy, the lady of the house and she is Sheila's mother."

When Timmy looked up to pay attention to his wife as she spoke, at once, he noticed Stacy. He could not believe what he was seeing. It was really her and she looked as amazing as she always used to. His heart raced at the sight of her. He had assured himself that he had let go of the feelings he had towards her. She looked beautiful, happy and cheerful. Indeed, age was not winning the battle. At that moment, again he admired his son's courage. If he had been just as firm as Charlie, he would have not missed living a happy life with his first love. If only he had, but because he did not, he could not help but envy Robin. The man was living his supposed life.

Intriguing! The son of the man who had broken her heart was about to marry her daughter. Now they were brought together once again; the unpredictability of fate. Typical of life; all bets were off. They had both never anticipated that their paths would cross again, in such a situation. Nonetheless, here they were, faced with an obligatory parental task.

THE END

Made in the USA
Lexington, KY
07 November 2019